Balancing Act

by Bernadette Kelly

STONE ARCH BOOKS
a capstone imprint

First published in the United States in 2011
by Stone Arch Books
A Capstone Imprint
151 Good Counsel Drive, P.O. Box 669
Mankato, Minnesota 56002
www.capstonepub.com

First published in Australia by Black Dog Books in 2007

Printed in the United States of America in Stevens Point, Wisconsin.
032010
005741WZF10

Library of Congress Cataloging-in-Publication Data is available on
the Library of Congress website.

Library Binding: 978-1-4342-3006-5

Summary: When Annie Boyd overschedules herself for two important events,
she has to figure out a way to make both commitments work.

Art Director: Kay Fraser
Graphic Designer: Emily Harris
Production Specialist: Michelle Biedscheid
Photo Credit: Capstone Studio/Karon Dubke, cover

Balancing Act

by Bernadette Kelly

I checked the chin strap on my riding helmet one more time. All around me, other Ridgeview Riding Club members were tacking up their horses for the afternoon's riding sessions.

The riding club grounds were located next to the racetrack in the town of Ridgeview. I looked out over the open space of the grounds. It had been divided into different areas.

To my left, colorful show jumps were set up. They would be taken apart and put away when the lessons were over. The games area was in front of me. Several plastic cones had been laid out, along with two empty drums. Inside the drums were wooden sticks with cloth flags attached to them.

Across the riding club grounds, in a less open area, I could see part of the cross-country course. The course was made up of unpainted wood, tires, and logs. The jumps almost blended into the surrounding landscape. I could only see the course and jumps in flashes among the trees, but I knew they were there.

To my right was the roped-off dressage area. That's where I was headed.

I stood next to my horse, Bobby. I held his reins in one hand and quickly checked the girth with the other. It was firm. I looked down at my riding club uniform. My jodhpurs, white shirt, deep blue sweater, and tie were clean and neat.

I hooked my foot into the stirrup. Then I jumped into the saddle. I gathered up the reins in both hands and squeezed my legs on Bobby's chestnut-colored sides.

"Let's go, boy," I said. "Time for our dressage lesson with Erica."

I was the first rider from my group to arrive for the dressage lesson. Our instructor, Erica, ran the only riding and boarding stable in town. I felt lucky to work part-time at her stables.

The only time I got to have a real lesson with Erica was at the riding club. I knew better than anyone that Erica was very busy. She was always giving paid lessons or training other people's horses. But once a month she spent her Sunday afternoon teaching dressage at the riding club.

Erica greeted me with a smile and gave Bobby a pat on his neck. Bobby leaned in to Erica's hand, and Erica reached up to find his favorite spot behind the ears.

I grinned. All horses liked Erica.

"How's he doing today?" Erica asked.

"He's doing great," I replied. "I'm feeling a lot more confident, too."

"I can tell," Erica said, nodding. "You've come a long way since you first joined the riding club. In fact, I think you might be almost ready to move up a level."

Erica looked up. The rest of the riders were approaching with their horses.

"Annie, I've been meaning to ask you something. Would you mind keeping the third Saturday of next month free?" she asked. "I'm taking Cadence to the National Dressage Championships. I thought you might like to be my groom for the event."

I stared at Erica with excitement. I didn't know what being a groom would require, but it didn't matter. I'd take any chance I could get to spend more time with horses.

"It's not too difficult," Erica explained.
"Just saddling and unsaddling for me. And
making sure that Cadence has food and water
in her paddock when I'm not around. I'd really
appreciate your help. And I'll pay you, of course."

"I'd love to," I answered right away. Helping
Erica at an event hardly seemed like work to me.

"Great," Erica replied, nodding. "I'm glad you
can do it."

The others arrived just as we finished talking.
Erica launched straight into the lesson.

The five riders in our group formed a circle
around Erica. Everyone made sure to stay out of
kicking distance of each other's horses.

I rode behind Austin Ryan. His horse was a
tall Thoroughbred mare named Cruise. Austin
considered himself a serious competitor. His goal
was to someday represent the country in the
Olympics.

In front of Cruise, Reese Moriarty kept her gray gelding, Jefferson, moving at a steady trot. Matt Snyder rode in front of Reese. Matt's horse was a lively Appaloosa named Bullet.

Jessica Coulson was the final member of the group. She rode a flashy black mare named Ripple. Jessica liked to remind everyone that the horse's real name was Ripponlea Duchess. She thought it sounded fancier.

As we all trotted around the arena, Erica watched carefully. She commented on each rider's position or rhythm.

"That's right, Annie," Erica called across the ring. "That's a good position for your hands. Just remember to maintain steady contact with your horse's mouth."

Proudly, I sat a little taller in the saddle. I thought about Erica's upcoming dressage competition.

All the best riders will be there, I thought. *Maybe if I watch how they do things, I can pick up a few tips for myself.*

I imagined Bobby in a dressage arena, strutting his stuff while the other riders watched in awe. My little chestnut horse, of no particular breed, making the horses with star-studded bloodlines look like amateurs.

Bobby came to a sudden halt. I was jolted back to reality and almost unseated. While I'd been daydreaming, Bobby had been inching closer and closer to Cruise.

I hadn't heard Erica tell the group to come to a halt. Everyone else had stopped except Bobby, who continued trotting — straight into Cruise's rump.

Luckily for me, Cruise wasn't startled and hadn't kicked out, like many horses would have. The mare just took a step sideways. Then she turned back to see what had collided with her.

Austin, though, was not happy with me. "Watch where you're going," he shouted. "I can't ride Cruise at the Interschool Equestrian Competition next month if she's injured."

"I'm really sorry," I said. "I wasn't paying attention."

"Yeah, no kidding," Jessica muttered with a smirk. Jessica was the snottiest person at the riding club. For some reason, she'd always seemed to have a grudge against me.

Erica looked disappointed. "Annie, you need to concentrate. If you can't, don't bother coming to the lesson," she said.

I blushed. All eyes were now on me. I lowered my head in embarrassment.

"I said I was sorry," I mumbled into my riding club sweater. "It won't happen again."

Erica gave me another look. I could tell she wasn't as impressed with my riding as she had been a few minutes ago. Then she sighed loudly and resumed the lesson.

This time, I made sure to give Erica my full attention.

At the end of the lesson, I quickly unsaddled Bobby. I put him in his yard near the arena. I made sure he had fresh water. Then I hurried off to find Austin.

I found him packing his tack into his parents' SUV. Cruise was already standing quietly in the horse trailer, waiting to go home.

Austin grinned when he saw me walking toward him. I realized with relief that he'd obviously forgiven me. Still, I gave him another sheepish apology.

"Don't worry about it," said Austin. "Cruise is fine. I don't think Erica was too impressed, though."

I quickly changed the subject. I didn't want to spend any more time discussing my embarrassing mistake.

"Hey, what was that event you mentioned during the lesson?" I asked. "Something about Interschool . . ."

"The Interschool Equestrian Competition," Austin replied. "I don't usually do it. It's not horse trials. But the school needed another rider to make up a team, and I was the only rider who could it. Jessica's doing it too, along with a couple of others from Swindley. Nobody else you'd know."

"I've never heard of an Interschool Equestrian Competition. What is it? I mean, what do you do?" I asked.

Austin closed the trunk. He turned to give me his full attention. "Each school can enter a team," he explained. "The teams are made up of either three or four people. Each rider chooses three activities to compete in, and every team has to have at least one rider in each of the activities. The activities are games, show ring, an obstacle course, dressage, and show jumping. Every year, a championship trophy is presented to the winning school."

"What activities are you competing in?" I asked.

"I'm doing dressage and show jumping, of course. But I can't decide between the others," Austin said. "I normally don't ride in any of them."

"So how do they decide on the winners?" I asked.

"Riders earn points depending on where they place in each individual event," he explained.

"The top three scores are used for each team in each event. Then the lowest score is discarded. My school won last year. Our manager thinks we'll win again this year. That will be back-to-back championships," Austin added proudly.

"Can any school enter?" I asked.

Austin shrugged. "I guess so," he replied. "There's a website you can look at." Austin pulled a piece of paper out of his pocket and scribbled down a website address.

Just then, Austin's mother walked over. They got into the SUV. "See you later, Annie," Austin said.

I waved after them. Their big SUV — horse trailer pulling along behind — drove through the riding club gate. Then it turned toward the road.

"Hey, Annie. Let's go," Reese called out.

I hurried over to where Reese was waiting with Jefferson, who was saddled and ready to go. I quickly gathered my tack and saddled Bobby as well.

It had been a warm day, but by late afternoon the air was growing cooler. Jefferson and Bobby ambled back home along the leafy trail on a loose rein.

My family and the Moriarty family lived next door to each other. Reese was my best friend. Sometimes Mrs. Moriarty brought both of our horses to riding club in the Moriartys' horse trailer. Today, Reese and I had decided to ride instead.

"Reese, have you ever competed in the Interschool Equestrian Competition?" I asked.

"No, I haven't," she replied. "I don't think Ridgeview High has ever had an equestrian team before."

"Why not?" I asked. "We'd have enough riders to get involved."

"You're probably right," Reese said, nodding in agreement. "There's the two of us and Matt. And I bet if we asked her, Laura would be interested."

"I'm sure she would be," I replied excitedly. Laura was Matt's older sister. "Matt and Laura are always up for games."

Reese turned to me. Her face looked like she had just made an amazing discovery. "You know, I don't think anyone has ever bothered to organize a team!" she exclaimed. "Can you believe that?"

I grinned. "Well, I think it's time somebody did," I said. "Leave it to me."

* * *

I decided to tackle my mother first. She worked at Ridgeview High. That could be a pain sometimes. Other times, though, it came in handy. I was hoping this would be one of those times. I waited until the trip home from school the next day to bring up my idea.

"Mom, do you know anything about the Interschool Equestrian Competition?" I asked.

"Not really," my mother answered. "I've seen a couple of flyers floating around the teachers' lounge. I asked about it once, but apparently it's not part of the athletics program."

"Well, that's pathetic. Why isn't it?" I asked angrily.

"I don't know, Annie. I guess it's just not something the school wants to encourage. All of the teachers are busy enough as it is, without taking on another commitment," my mother said. "Besides, you and your friends have plenty of opportunities to ride at home and at the riding club. I don't think this is a big loss for you."

"But this is different!" I argued. "This is a school sport I'd actually want to do. We have teams for practically every other sport. And we're always doing boring stuff like hosting swim meets."

It didn't seem fair to me that my mother was just ignoring my idea right away. She hadn't even given it a chance.

"We'd have enough riders to enter a riding team," I told her. "Can't you at least ask the principal about it?"

My mother frowned. "Annie, if you want to have a school equestrian team, you'll need to ask Mrs. Davies yourself. You don't get special treatment just because I work at the school," she said.

Disappointed, I turned away. I stared out through the car window. Fences and grassy hills flew past the window.

My mother softened. "I didn't say you couldn't give it a try, sweetie," she said. "I just don't want you to be too disappointed if she says no. Our teaching staff is already stretched to the limit as it is."

"Well, I'm going to try anyway," I said stubbornly. "It doesn't hurt to ask."

I arrived at the principal's office early the next morning. Mrs. Davies's door was closed, and a DO NOT DISTURB sign hung from the handle. I thought about coming back later, but decided against it. It had taken all my courage to get to the office in the first place.

A row of three chairs lined the wall outside Mrs. Davies's office. A constant stream of students and teachers walked past.

I sat down on the middle chair to wait. People walking by shot me curious glances. I wondered if they thought I was waiting outside the principal's office because I was in trouble.

Embarrassed, I stood up and pretended to read a nearby bulletin board. I was reading the details of the school's discipline policy for the third time when the door finally opened. Mrs. Davies appeared in the doorway.

"Can I help you with something?" the principal asked.

I swallowed nervously. I tried to remember everything I'd planned to say. But my mind had gone blank.

"I . . . I wanted to ask you something," I stuttered.

That was a terrible start, I thought to myself.

Mrs. Davies ushered me into her office. The principal sat down at her desk. I kept standing until she motioned for me to take a seat in the chair across from her desk.

"You're Annie, right?" she asked. "You're Susan Boyd's daughter."

I nodded. "Yes, that's me," I said quietly.

Mrs. Davies glanced briefly at her watch. "Well, what's up, Annie?" she asked. "I have a meeting, so you'll have to be quick."

I cleared my throat. "We want to enter a team for the Interschool Equestrian Competition," I finally blurted out. "It's next month."

"I see," Mrs. Davies said carefully. "And who exactly is 'we'?"

"Me . . . and some other kids at this school who ride," I said. "There's not a lot of us, but we do have enough to make a team." Then I remembered the words I had practiced earlier. "We want to represent our school in our chosen sport," I finished.

Mrs. Davies pursed her lips, staring at me thoughtfully.

"Annie," she began. Then she paused for a moment.

I could already tell from the tone of the principal's voice that I wasn't going to like what she had to say.

"I've looked into having an equestrian team before. It's complicated," she explained. "We have a curriculum that the school is required to follow. There's just no room in the day for horse-riding practice. Then there's the problem of uniforms. They require funding. And you also would need a staff member to supervise and act as team manager. All the staff members are busy as it is."

I stared at Mrs. Davies. *This is so unfair,* I thought to myself. *The school has enough time and money to send kids to swim meets and football games and other athletic events. We even have a debate team. If the school can do that for other activities, why can't they do the same for the horse riders?*

The principal picked up a pen from her desk. She was waiting for me to leave. Mrs. Davies's fingers clicked the top of the pen in then out again. *Click, click, click.* The pen top went up and down several times. Then Mrs. Davies checked her watch again and stood up.

"I'm sorry, Annie, but I really do have to leave," she said, pushing back her chair.

Is that it? I thought. *I wasted my time worrying about this meeting for nothing?*

I wasn't ready to leave. Mrs. Davies obviously noticed my stubborn look. She sighed loudly.

"Annie . . ." she began.

"What if I get all the information together for you to look at?" I interrupted. I had to do something to get Mrs. Davies to think about the idea. "I could come up with a plan to show you how the equestrian team would work. I'll include all the details. I'm sure my friends would help."

"I'll look at it, Annie," said the principal, moving toward the door and motioning for me to leave the office. "But I'm not making any promises."

I jumped out of the seat with a grin. "Thank you, Mrs. Davies," I said. "You won't regret it!"

"Maybe we can look at a team for next year," Mrs. Davies said as she left.

My grin vanished almost instantly. *Not next year*, I thought. *This year.*

* * *

I went to the library after my last class of the day. I dug into my pocket and found the crumpled piece of paper Austin had given me. Written on it was the website address for the Interschool Equestrian Competition.

The meeting with Mrs. Davies had only made me more determined. I needed to do this. There had to be some way that I could change the principal's mind. She had to let us enter a team for the upcoming event.

I found a set of rules for the competition online and printed it out. The website also had information about other horse events happening around the country. Plus it had links to some interesting articles.

I noticed an article about a rescue shelter for mistreated horses. There were several photographs of sad-looking horses. Their hipbones stuck out and sores covered their bodies. I memorized the name of the shelter — Hopedale.

I'll come back and read the article another time, I thought. *Right now I just need to focus on the Interschool info. I don't have any time to waste.*

When I got home, I called Reese and told her about my meeting with Mrs. Davies.

"Hey, what are you up to right now?" I asked when I'd filled her in. "Can you come over?

I need help coming up with some ideas for Mrs. Davies."

"But I thought she didn't go for it," Reese said. "Not this year, anyway."

"Well, we're just going to have to convince her," I replied.

"I'll be right over," said Reese.

* * *

Reese and I stretched out on my living-room floor. We'd both changed out of our school uniforms into jeans and T-shirts. We could see the field behind my house through the oversized living-room window in front of us.

My dad had bought the small farm when he had been offered a new job as an agent for Ridgeview Real Estate.

That was almost a year ago. Back then, I hadn't wanted to move away from the city and all my friends. Now, though, I couldn't imagine living anywhere else. I smiled as I gazed out the window.

Bobby and my father's sheep were grazing in their paddock, while my dog — an energetic little Jack Russell named Jonesy — trotted across the lawn.

I set the program on the floor. The event was being held at Woodside, a large equestrian center about forty minutes away from Ridgeview. Reese and I both cringed when we saw the event's entry fee prices. It cost fifty dollars per rider, plus another twenty dollars for the team's entry fee!

"It's expensive," Reese said nervously. "I've never been to a riding club event that charges that much."

I nodded. Somehow, I didn't think Mrs. Davies was going to be too happy forking over that kind of money. Not for a team of four kids.

"Maybe that's why the school sticks with bigger athletic events and swim meets," said Reese. "They're probably a lot cheaper, and the school can send more kids."

I frowned at Reese. "That kind of thinking isn't going to get us to the event," I told her. "We have to focus on the positives. Otherwise, how are we going to convince Mrs. Davies?"

But privately, I agreed with Reese. Mrs. Davies might have had a point.

In addition to the entry fees, the horses had to be brought to the event. "How will we get the horses there?" I asked.

"My mom can take Jefferson and Bobby," Reese suggested. "And I bet Mr. Snyder would be willing to take the other horses."

"We also have to find a staff member to be our team manager," I said.

"Let's ask your mom," Reese said.

"I don't know," I replied. "She didn't seem too interested when I brought it up on the ride home."

"She'll do it," Reese said confidently.

I wasn't so sure. Reese seemed to think everything would just take care of itself. But the more I found out about the whole Interschool Equestrian Competition, the more worried I was. There was a lot more to organizing it than I'd originally thought.

Reese kept reading from the pages I'd printed out, making comments as she went. "At least we won't have to take time off school. It's on a Saturday," she said. "Oh, look, Jake is sponsoring the event!" Reese pointed to the logo for Jake's Traveling Tack Shop at the bottom of the information sheet. Reese had been buying tack from Jake for years.

I suddenly had an idea. "That's it!" I yelled, grinning. "We can get sponsors. Mrs. Davies can't say no if we find a way to pay for the whole thing."

"Well, we obviously can't ask Jake," said Reese. "He's already sponsoring the event. What other businesses could we ask?"

I was way ahead of her.

"Ridgeview Real Estate!" I announced, feeling proud of my great idea. My father worked there, and Matt's dad owned the company. What could be easier? It was perfect.

When I arrived at the stables the next
afternoon, Erica was already riding Cadence in
the indoor arena. I watched for a minute before
getting to work. Erica always looked so perfectly
balanced and in control when she rode. She
made it all look so easy.

I clearly remembered when Erica had first
brought Cadence to the stables. The young mare
had been inexperienced and skittish. Cadence
had literally jumped at her own shadow. She'd
needed hours of training.

Erica's skill and patience with the beautiful chestnut mare was really paying off. Cadence was turning into an amazing dressage horse.

I had heard Erica using a range of terms for the different movements. I still got a little confused when I heard some of them. She used words like leg yields, shoulder-ins, half-halts, and flying-changes. I didn't know what half of the movements were, let alone how to ride them.

I watched for another minute as Erica and Cadence cantered down the long side of the arena. Then I went off to start cleaning the stalls.

As I worked, I planned my argument. My father was picking me up after work. I needed to talk to him. I'd thought about the idea a lot. I couldn't think of a single reason why my father and Mr. Snyder wouldn't agree to sponsor our team for the event.

I finished cleaning the stables. Then I fed the horses and put each of them away in their boxes.

Using saddle soap, leather oil, and a fair amount of elbow grease, I started working my way through four saddles and their matching bridles. I also polished stirrup irons and bits. Then I wiped the girths with a towel and warm water.

Erica appeared in the doorway and nodded in approval. "Good job, Annie. Thanks for your hard work. You can head home now if you want," she said.

"My dad's picking me up," I told Erica. "He should be here soon. I'll just keep working till he gets here."

Erica sat down on a nearby bench and watched me work.

"I saw you riding," I told her. "Cadence looks great."

Erica smiled. "Yeah, she's starting to really get the hang of things now," she agreed. "I'm looking forward to testing her skills at the National

Dressage Championships. You're still planning on coming, right?"

"Of course," I replied. "I wouldn't miss it." I hung the last clean girth on a hook. Just then, my father pulled into the driveway.

My dad seemed like he was in a good mood when I got in the car. He smiled at me cheerfully as I buckled my seatbelt.

"So how are things?" he asked. He pulled out of Erica's driveway and turned toward home.

I turned to my dad and smiled. "Things are pretty good. I've been working on a project for school," I said.

"Me too!" my dad exclaimed. "Well, for work, I mean."

"What's your project?" I asked.

My father's smile widened. "I just sold one of the most expensive houses in the area!" he said proudly. "But more importantly, Ray Snyder is promoting me to sales manager."

"Wow!" I said. "That's great! Actually, Dad, about my project . . ."

My father wasn't finished. "I think we need to celebrate tonight," he interrupted. "I'm taking you and your mother out for dinner."

He turned into our driveway and drove up to the house. "I can't wait to tell your mom," he said. He parked the car in the garage and hurried inside.

Disappointed, I slumped in my seat for a moment. *I should have asked him right away,* I thought. *I guess I'll just have to wait and ask him tonight while we're all having dinner.*

* * *

Later that night, a young waiter showed my parents and me to a table at The Ridge. It was Ridgeview's only restaurant, located inside the local hotel. The owners had done their best to make the place look like an upscale restaurant. It had crisp white tablecloths, dim lighting, and candles burning in glass holders on the tables. The restaurant was at the back of the hotel. I could hear a faint hum of conversation and the clink of glasses from the main bar.

Both of my parents had dressed up for the evening. I had settled for a cute pair of jeans and my new pink shirt. I figured that was dressy enough.

This outfit would have made me feel underdressed when I lived in the city. Not anymore. None of my Ridgeview friends, except maybe Jessica, cared much about clothes. These days, I didn't either.

I had been to plenty of fancy restaurants when we'd lived in the city. They always had tiny servings and I was still hungry after three courses. I hoped The Ridge wasn't going to be like that.

The chicken I ordered turned out to be plenty big enough. My parents had ordered a more sophisticated meal of snapper arranged on a bed of seasoned potatoes.

The fish had arrived whole, with the eyes still staring up from the table. I couldn't look at them. Those fish eyes staring up at me creeped me out big time.

Dad spent the whole meal describing how he had made his big sale.

It must have been a great deal, I thought. *I can't ever remember seeing Dad this happy.*

Finally, my mother reached across and touched my hand briefly. "You're quiet, Annie," she said.

"I have some good news of my own," I said with a shaky laugh. "Actually, it's just a great idea at this point. Dad, I think you might be interested in it."

My father placed his knife and fork on his empty plate. Then he gave me his full attention. "I'm all ears, Annie," he said cheerfully.

"Well, do you remember that project I was telling you about? The one for school?" I asked.

My father nodded, wiping at the side of his mouth with a napkin.

"I thought Ridgeview Real Estate might like to be a sponsor," I said. "What do you think, Dad?"

My mother was suddenly interested. "Project?" she asked. "What project are you talking about?"

"It must be a big project if you're looking for sponsors," said my father.

My parents listened as I outlined my plan to enter a team in the Interschool Equestrian Competition.

"But, Annie, I thought Mrs. Davies only told you to get some information together. Don't you think you're getting a little ahead of yourself?" my mom asked gently.

I shook my head. "Don't you see, Mom?" I said. "I have a really good plan. And if it's already been organized and paid for, then Mrs. Davies will have no reason to say no."

My mother didn't seem convinced. I turned to my father. He didn't seem as impressed by my idea as I'd hoped he would be. When he shook his head, my stomach dropped.

"I can't ask Ray Snyder for favors right now, Annie," Dad said. "He just gave me a promotion. I'd look greedy if I started making more demands right away."

"But, Dad, Mr. Snyder is involved with the riding club too," I argued. "And Matt would be on the team. He'd probably be glad to help."

But my father wasn't listening. "I'm sorry, Annie. The timing's just not right," he said.

"But I'll tell you what. Why don't you present your plan to the school principal anyway, for next year? I'm sure Ridgeview Real Estate would sponsor you by then."

"Yeah, sure, Dad," I answered softly.

Frustrated, I kicked the table leg, making the candle flutter and my parents' wine glasses tremble. I pretended not to notice my mother's warning look.

* * *

By the next day, I had almost given up on entering a team in the Interschool event. Then I had another idea. Maybe we could get everyone at school to sponsor the team and raise money for charity at the same time.

Hopefully everyone else won't think the new idea is lame. It's worth a try, I thought. *It might be just what we need to convince Mrs. Davies to get the team to the event.*

To my surprise, Reese, Matt, and Laura agreed to the charity fundraising idea when I brought it up during lunch.

"Mrs. Davies will love it," said Laura. "She's really big on helping the poor and stuff. Remember when we sang carols to raise money for the hospital?"

Matt made a face. "Good thing we weren't singing to the patients," he said. "They would have ended up sicker than when we started."

Reese hit Matt on the arm. "There's nothing wrong with helping other people," she told him.

"I know, I know," Matt said. "I'm not saying that. I just would have rather done anything else than sing."

"Do you think the kids at school would actually sponsor us, though?" I asked.

"Of course they will," said Matt. "Mrs. Davies will make them."

"She would, if she needed to," added Reese. "And the Ridgeview High kids will be into it. They're always raising money for something."

"We need to have a few things figured out before we talk to Mrs. Davies again," I said. "I don't want to give her any reason to say no. First, I thought we could wear our school sweaters with our riding club jodhpurs. That way we don't need new uniforms."

Everyone nodded in agreement. They all seemed fine with that idea.

"And we can practice at home after school. That way the teachers can't complain about us missing out on class time," I continued.

"Did you ask your mom about being the team manager yet?" asked Reese. "We can't compete if we don't have a manager."

I chewed on my thumbnail. I'd been putting off asking her in the hopes that Reese would forget. My mother was so busy with schoolwork all the time. It never seemed like the right time to ask her. Plus, she hadn't seemed too happy about the idea in the first place.

"Not yet," I admitted.

Reese rolled her eyes and sighed. "I'll ask her myself," she said.

"Good idea," I said with a smile. "She's probably more likely to say yes to you, anyway. Now, we have to choose our activities. We need three each."

I picked up a pen to fill out the entry form. I figured that if I filled out all the details, there'd be nothing left for Mrs. Davies to do except sign and send in the forms.

It seemed like everybody wanted to do games. Matt picked the obstacle course and show jumping for his second and third choices. After games, Laura asked to do dressage and show jumping. Reese decided to sign up for the obstacle course, dressage, and games.

That just left me. I signed up for games, show jumping, and the obstacle course. Those were my best activities. Then I read back over the entry form and noticed a problem.

"Nobody signed up for show ring," I said. "The rules say that each team has to have a rider competing in every event."

The others all looked uncomfortable. It was clear no one wanted to do the show ring, even if it was just this one time.

I didn't bother trying to convince Matt or Laura. They were both nuts about games. I knew neither of them would be caught dead in a show ring.

I glanced hopefully at Reese. I knew Reese had been to shows in the past. But she shook her head. "Don't look at me," she said firmly.

"I hate shows. I only ever went because my mother wanted me to."

"But I don't have any idea how to compete in a show," I complained.

Reese was silent.

I stared at three stubborn faces. If I didn't do the show activity, the team wouldn't happen.

"Oh, all right," I snapped. "I'll do it."

I crossed out "games" next to my name and wrote "show ring" instead.

The team was organized. Now all I had to do was convince Mrs. Davies.

Jonesy followed me as I carried an armful of hay out to Bobby's paddock. Bobby spotted the hay as I walked up. He wandered closer to the gate.

"Hey, boy," I called out.

I threw the hay over the fence. Bobby nosed around, searching for a tasty bite, before he began to chew.

I wondered what was going through my horse's head. What made one part of the hay any different from another? It all looked the same to me. Besides, he'd end up eating the whole pile anyway.

A couple of sheep wandered closer, hoping for some of the hay, but Bobby wasn't in the mood to share. He pinned his russet ears back against his head and turned to glare at the sheep. Jonesy's sharp bark at the sheep added a second threat. The sheep trotted away in alarm.

I laughed. Bobby was a terrible bully to my dad's sheep, but I was more than happy for him to keep his food to himself — especially since I had bought the hay using my hard-earned money. There was plenty of grass in Bobby's paddock, but I liked to give him a treat once in a while. Sometimes I brought him an apple, too, but not today.

I had been trying to save up enough money for new tack, but it seemed there was always some little thing that Bobby needed. So far this month I'd already had to buy horse wormer and a new lead rope. The clip on the old one had snapped. And I had to pay to have Bobby's hooves trimmed and his shoes reset every six weeks.

I'm lucky I have my part-time job at the stables, I thought. *Owning a horse is great, but it sure isn't cheap.*

I stood watching Bobby munch on his hay for another few minutes. Then I said goodbye, scooped Jonesy into my arms, and headed back to the house.

Inside, my mother was talking to someone on the phone.

"Of course I'll do it," she said, glancing over at me. "I'll mark the date on my calendar right now. No, it's not too much work. In fact, I'm excited about it. I don't know why Annie didn't ask me herself."

I snuck up to my bedroom. I had a pretty good idea who was on the phone and what they were talking about.

A few minutes later, Mom was at my bedroom door, holding the phone out to me. "Reese wants to talk to you," she said. She was trying to sound stern, but I could see a hint of a smile around her eyes and mouth.

I took the phone sheepishly, grinning at her as she left the room.

"She said yes. I told you she would," were Reese's first words. "There's just one tiny thing. I don't think she knows that we don't have permission for the team yet."

"You didn't tell her?" I asked. I gasped. "Reese, what if we don't get permission? Mom won't be happy, and we'll both be in trouble."

"No we won't. Mrs. Davies will agree. I know she will," said Reese confidently.

I hung up and slumped back onto my bed. I couldn't put it off any longer. I needed to talk to Mrs. Davies tomorrow. I wished I was as sure as Reese that everything would all work out.

I thought about how excited the other three team members were about the Interschool event. This whole thing had gotten a lot bigger than I had expected. What had I gotten myself into? There was only one thing I knew for sure — there were going to be a lot of disappointed people if my plan didn't work out.

* * *

The next morning, Matt, Reese, and I knocked on the principal's office door. Laura was home from school that day with a sore throat, so she couldn't make it.

I had been counting on Laura, who was a senior, to present our argument to Mrs. Davies. I thought she might have better luck. But now it looked like we'd just have to do it on our own.

Mrs. Davies looked surprised when she opened her door. After a second, she invited us into her office. The principal took a seat behind her desk and pointed to a group of chairs stacked in the corner. We each took a chair from the pile and sat down on the other side of the desk.

"So," said Mrs. Davies. "To what do I owe the pleasure of this visit?" She didn't look at all pleased.

It's too early, I thought. *She's not in a very good mood. Oh, I never should have started this.*

Mrs. Davies was waiting. She started to look annoyed.

"Um. Well, we're here because . . . I came to see you about the Interschool Equestrian Competition last week," I began.

"Yes, you did," Mrs. Davies said. She nodded, sounding bored. "If I remember correctly, I told you to gather some information for next year."

I swallowed hard. *Here goes nothing*, I thought.

"I got all the information like I promised," I told her. "I even put a team together."

I looked toward the other two. They were nodding.

"And Laura Snyder wants to be on the team too," I added. Even though Laura couldn't be there, I was hoping her support would help change Mrs. Davies's opinion.

"That's great," said Mrs. Davies. "Leave me the details. I'll put it on the schedule for discussion at the next school board meeting."

The principal reached over her desk and picked up a load of papers.

Before I could say anything else, Matt started talking. "We don't need to wait until next year, Mrs. Davies," he said. "We found a way to cover all the expenses and raise money for charity at the same time."

Mrs. Davies suddenly sat up a little straighter. "You did?" she asked, sounding surprised.

"Yep," said Matt, nodding. "Actually, it was all Annie's idea. We thought we could find sponsors for the event. Friends and family, and kids from school. Everyone could pledge money for us to ride at the event. After the event is over, we can decide which charity we want to donate the money to."

Mrs. Davies was starting to look interested. "A charity?" she asked. "I didn't realize you could raise money for charity by riding horses."

I handed over my carefully written proposal. It showed all the details of the Interschool Equestrian Event.

Is she really thinking about it? I wondered.

Mrs. Davies flipped through the pages. "Well, you've certainly done a lot of research," she said slowly.

We all sat quietly. Mrs. Davies read through the plan. When she looked up, her face gave nothing away.

I held my breath. I wasn't sure whether I wanted to hear the answer or not.

Mrs. Davies finally spoke. "Have you decided on a charity?" she asked.

"No, we haven't decided on a charity yet. But . . . does that mean we can do it?" Matt asked carefully.

"I think so," said Mrs. Davies, nodding. "We still need to figure out the specifics. You've put a lot of work into this. I'll get some sponsor forms organized for you. This school is always happy to help students raise money for charity."

A knowing glance passed between Reese and Matt. Then they turned and looked at me with told-you-so looks on their faces. I laughed. For once, I didn't mind being proven wrong.

I had a charity in mind. But I'd keep that to myself for now.

We were going to the Interschool Equestrian Competition. We were Ridgeview High's very first equestrian team!

The next few weeks flew by. Before I knew
it, it was riding club day again. The Interschool
Equestrian Competition was only a week away.

"We really need to find time to practice," I told
Reese and Matt. We were waiting for the rest of
the group to arrive for gear check.

"Practice for what?" asked a voice from
behind us.

Reese, Matt, and I turned. Jessica Coulson was
standing behind us.

"Practice for the Interschool Equestrian Competition," Matt replied confidently. "There's going to be a team from Ridgeview High competing this year. And we're planning to take that trophy from you Swindley kids."

Jessica frowned and turned to Reese. "I guess you'll be competing in the show ring," she said with a sigh. "After all, Jefferson is the only horse out of all of yours that's even close to being show quality. The rest of you would just be an embarrassment."

Jessica was being her normal stuck-up self, but something in her voice sounded different. It almost seemed like she was afraid she might lose.

"Is that so?" Reese asked mysteriously.

Reese and I exchanged a secret smile. We didn't tell Jessica that Bobby and I were the ones who would be competing against her in the show ring.

I gathered up the reins in my left hand. With my right hand, I rubbed Bobby's neck.

Bobby and I had never been near a show ring. I was sure Jessica would beat us. Still, for the first time since I had started riding, I wished I knew more about showing. It would have been nice to at least give Jessica a run for her money.

Matt didn't seem to notice the tension between us girls. He was too busy telling Austin all about the sponsorship arrangements. We'd already raised a lot of money for charity.

"All the kids at school want to see us bring home the trophy," Matt said, laughing. "But most of them have no idea how a horse competition actually works."

I noticed Austin stiffen when Matt mentioned the trophy. He glanced over at Jessica quickly.

They really want to win, I thought. *I guess I can't blame them, though. So do we.*

I noticed a weird feeling between the Swindley team and the team from Ridgeview. None of us were acting normal.

Things didn't get any better at lunchtime, either. Mrs. Coulson and Reese's mom were working in the lunch shed together when I walked up to the counter for lunch.

Jessica must have told her mother about the Ridgeview team. Mrs. Coulson started questioning me as soon as she saw me.

"So Ridgeview High has a team in this year's Interschool competition?" she asked.

Mrs. Coulson was dressed perfectly, as usual. She was wearing a leather jacket and expensive jeans.

I mumbled a reply and quickly moved up the line. But Mrs. Coulson wasn't finished. She turned to Mrs. Moriarty. "It's nice to see the local school participating," Jessica's mom said smugly, "but you have to know that Swindley is going to win. After all, we have a team of extremely talented riders. And our horses are all excellent quality. The Swindley students deserve that trophy."

I looked down at my riding boots to hide my amused grin. It was easy to see where Jessica got her attitude. Mrs. Coulson was exactly like her daughter. They were both super-competitive.

Reese's mother was almost as bad. "We'll see who deserves the trophy after it's won," said Mrs. Moriarty. "Besides, anything can happen on the day of the competition. You've been around horses long enough to know that by now."

I moved away from Mrs. Moriarty and Mrs. Coulson as they continued arguing. Carrying my lunch, I walked over to join Reese and Matt.

Austin and Jessica normally sat with us to eat lunch, but today they had moved outside. There was definitely some tension between our two teams. And now the adults were getting in on it too! I was starting to wonder where all this rivalry would lead.

"Mom's going to be worse than usual now," Reese muttered before taking a bite of her turkey sandwich. "If I'm riding in the same events as Jessica, my mom's going to be extra competitive. I'll never hear the end of it if I don't beat Jessica."

"But it's all so silly," I said. "I don't understand why everyone's being so competitive. I just want the team to have fun."

Reese nodded. "Tell me about it," she said. "Friendly rivalry between schools is one thing. But this is ridiculous."

"Oh, they'll get over it," Matt said confidently. "Besides, as long as we all enjoy ourselves, who cares who wins?"

I agreed with Matt. But it looked like we were the only ones not worried about winning. Everyone else seemed determined to make a big deal of the competition between Ridgeview and Swindley. I finished my lunch in worried silence. I hadn't expected this.

* * *

The Ridgeview team, including our horses, met at Reese's house the following afternoon. We were trying to squeeze in a much-needed practice before the Interschool event. The Moriartys' farm had plenty of space for us. We'd be able to practice all the different events.

I was the only one who wouldn't be competing in games at the Interschool event. I was happy to practice anyway. Games were always fun. Laura had also designed an obstacle course for us to practice on.

First, the riders had to open and close a gate while on horseback. Then, we had to have our horses walk across a makeshift "bridge." Laura had made it by pushing together wooden boards on the ground. We also rode through imaginary "water," which was really just a bright blue plastic tarp.

Thankfully, none of the horses spooked at any of the tasks. Matt, Reese, and I were pretty sure that we had nailed the obstacle course part of the competition.

Nobody practiced dressage or show jumping. We decided that since we'd done both the day before at the riding club, it wasn't necessary.

Everyone else started getting ready to leave for home. But I didn't think we were done. "What about showing?" I asked. "We haven't practiced that at all yet."

"What about it?" Matt asked. "You don't need to practice showing. It's just walking and trotting around in a circle. Even a beginner can handle doing that."

Reese and Laura were both nodding. None of them took showing seriously.

"That's not fair," I complained. "I got stuck doing it. I don't know anything about showing. Don't I have to get Bobby's mane braided or something? He can't go in a show ring looking like this!"

The others all looked at Bobby. He looked the same as he always did. He had a dark chestnut coat with matching mane and tail, and a white blaze running down his nose. He looked adorable. But even I had to admit he was looking a little scruffy.

I loved Bobby. But I was thinking about Jessica's beautiful show horse, Ripple. Ripple was always perfectly groomed. Her black coat always had a glossy sheen. There was never a single hair out of place.

I knew that Jessica would have Ripple washed and groomed perfectly for the Interschool event. I wanted Bobby to look nice, but I had no clue how to start getting him ready.

Matt just shrugged. "Don't ask me," he said helplessly. "I don't have any idea how to get ready for a show."

Laura looked blank too. I turned to Reese.

"My mom always gets Jefferson ready for shows," Reese said apologetically. "I just ride him when we get there."

"Don't you worry, Annie," a voice from behind me said. "I'll have that horse looking like a champion in no time."

I looked back to see Mrs. Moriarty walking up with a tray of drinks. She'd obviously overheard us talking.

I hesitated. I didn't want to bother Mrs. Moriarty. But on the other hand, I knew I couldn't say no. I needed all the help I could get.

"Bring him over here the day before the event," Mrs. Moriarty said. She handed each of us a glass of lemonade. Then she added, "We'll show the Coulsons what a winning show horse looks like."

I swallowed awkwardly. Reese smirked at me.

It looked like the decision had already been made. Reese's mom was going to help me turn Bobby into a show horse for the Interschool event whether I wanted her to or not.

I knew I should feel grateful. After all, I'd been asking for help. But it was pretty clear that Mrs. Moriarty had a problem with Mrs. Coulson. She was using me to solve it.

At the stables later that week, I watched as Erica finished exercising Cadence. When she finished her dressage practice, she rode over to where I stood.

She spoke quickly as she dismounted. "Hose her down, dry her off, and put her away for the night," she said. Then she handed me the reins.

Erica had been working the mare between her scheduled lessons. Sometimes it was the only free time she had during the day.

As I walked away, Erica turned her attention to her next customer. It was a young boy riding a white horse. Today was the first time I had seen the pair at Erica's stables.

I walked Cadence over to the outdoor wash rack and pulled out a hose. Then I started to hose her all over. Cadence was sweaty after the riding session with Erica. She seemed to enjoy the bath. She stood on three legs, looking relaxed. She lowered her head to sniff the ground. The cool water rinsed over her back and neck.

I turned the water pressure down to a trickle. Even when I let it run down Cadence's face, she didn't seem bothered. All she did was grab the hose with her mouth and swallow a few mouthfuls. I wasn't sure whether Cadence was playing with the hose or actually trying to take a drink.

Finally, I used a sweat scraper to remove the extra water from Cadence's coat. After she had been dried off, I put her blanket on her. Then I put her in her stall.

While Cadence was digging into her evening meal, Erica joined me at the stall door. I was checking the mare over one last time over before I left for the night.

"Thanks for doing that," Erica said gratefully.

"No problem," I replied. "I'm happy to help out. I love Cadence."

I could tell Erica was checking to make sure that I had taken good care of her horse. I wasn't at all offended. I knew that I'd probably do the same thing if I let someone else take care of Bobby.

"So, are you ready for this weekend?" Erica asked.

"Definitely," I said. "I'm really looking forward to it."

Erica nodded and turned to walk away. "Great," she called back over her shoulder. "I promise I won't make you work too hard. There might even be time for you to look around. I think there are a couple of other events happening at Woodside this weekend too, so there should be plenty to see."

It took me a minute to realize that Erica and I hadn't been talking about the same thing.

The words *Woodside* and *this weekend* flashed through my mind. I had been thinking about the Interschool event. With a feeling of panic, I realized that Erica had been talking about something else entirely. The National Dressage Championships.

This can't be happening, I thought frantically. *How could I not have checked the dates?*

My face felt hot. What was I going to do? I had been so busy trying to organize a team for the Interschool Equestrian Competition that

I had double-booked my time. The Interschool competition was happening on the same day as the National Dressage Championships. And at the exact same place!

* * *

When I got home from work that afternoon, Mrs. Moriarty's big SUV was parked in our driveway.

I figured Mrs. Moriarty and my mother were inside. They were probably talking about the upcoming competition. I knew they'd want to tell me all the details as soon as I walked in the door. After my realization at the stables that day, I was in no mood to hear about it. I needed time to think.

I rummaged through my backpack. I pulled out the apple I hadn't eaten at lunch. I dropped my bag on the front porch. Then I turned and headed out to Bobby's paddock.

Right now I wish I'd never heard of the Interschool event, I thought.

Bobby munched on the apple. Juice dribbled down the sides of his chin. I thoughtfully stroked my horse's ears.

How am I going to get out of this one? I thought miserably. *It's not like I can go back on my promise to help at the National Dressage Championships. I can't let Erica down so close to the event. She'd never forgive me.*

On the other hand, there was no way I could pull out of the equestrian team either. Without me, the team wouldn't have enough riders. Plus, I had been the one who had started the team in the first place.

I knew Mrs. Davies wouldn't be impressed if I backed out at the last minute. The entry fees had already been paid. Transportation for the horses was arranged. Canceling now wasn't an option.

I sat down on the ground beside the paddock fence. Bobby nosed my hand, hoping I might have another apple hidden there. When he didn't find anything, he wandered away to graze.

I lay back on the prickly grass. The light was fading. I would have to go in soon. My mother would be wondering where I was.

As I lay there, I thought about the sponsor money that had been promised to the team for charity. If we didn't compete, there'd be no charity donation.

I can't quit the team, I thought. *But what am I going to tell Erica?*

I gazed up at the sky, hoping for a sign to help solve my problem. A few stars were starting to appear. I knew that later there would be thousands.

The clear night sky was one thing I didn't take for granted after moving from the city. Every night, thousands of glittering lights filled the sky. I wondered what the stars would look like from the darkness of outer space.

That thought suddenly stopped me. I sat straight up.

Space. That was it!

Both competitions were being held at the same space. Reese had told me all about Woodside. It was a huge equestrian complex, with enough space for hundreds of horses.

I can do both! I thought. *I can help Erica and compete in my events. I'll have to be really organized, but I'm sure I can make it work.*

I jumped up from the ground and quickly wiped the grass and dust off my jeans. "See you later, boy!" I called out to Bobby.

The horse flicked an ear in my direction, but he didn't look up. He kept on grazing.

With my new plan, I wouldn't even have to tell Erica about my mistake — or anyone, for that matter. They all had enough to think about already.

Besides, it was a perfect plan, and I could handle it all on my own.

No problem!

Chapter Eight

The night before the Interschool Competition, I brought Bobby over to the Moriartys' barn. Mrs. Moriarty was going to help me get him ready for the show ring. In the morning, she'd take both Bobby and Jefferson to the event.

When I got there, Mrs. Moriarty took over. All I really did was hold Bobby. First, Reese's mother scrubbed every inch of Bobby with shampoo. She paid special attention to his tail. She told me more than once that I really should wash my horse more often.

I didn't want to upset Mrs. Moriarty, so I just nodded. In the past, a good grooming had always been enough to keep Bobby looking nice.

She rinsed, conditioned, and then rinsed again. Then Mrs. Moriarty dried Bobby off. She pulled out the clippers. Bobby eyed them nervously. Mrs. Moriarty held them close to Bobby, with the motor buzzing. Soon, he relaxed enough for her to begin.

Mrs. Moriarty started at Bobby's feet and worked her way up. She trimmed off long tufts of hair from Bobby's fetlocks. Before I could say anything, she moved up to his face. She buzzed off the whiskers around his chin and muzzle.

I was worried about this. "Aren't the whiskers supposed to help horses feel things around them?" I asked nervously. I didn't want poor Bobby bumping into stuff.

Mrs. Moriarty nodded. "You're right," she said, "but in a show class the judges want to see the horse looking neat and tidy. That includes clipping off straggly whiskers. Don't worry, they'll grow back soon."

Then Mrs. Moriarty started braiding Bobby's tail. When she was finished braiding, Mrs. Moriarty carefully tucked the messy end back up into the braid and out of sight.

I was impressed by how elegant Bobby instantly looked with the tightly braided tail. He was starting to look like a real show horse.

Bobby's mane took a lot longer to braid. First, Mrs. Moriarty used a comb to divide Bobby's mane into even pieces. Then she carefully sectioned off each strip with a rubber band. She tightly braided each strip down, starting at the top of the mane. Finally, she rolled each braid up into a tight little ball at the base of his mane. She used a needle and thread to sew it all into place.

"We really should have pulled Bobby's mane, but there's no time now," Mrs. Moriarty said.

When she explained that pulling a horse's mane meant thinning it out by teasing and yanking out the hair, I was glad we didn't have time for it. It sounded really painful. I knew I wouldn't have wanted my own hair treated like that.

After the braiding was finished, we covered Bobby with a blanket and a hood. Mrs. Moriarty added a tail bag, borrowed from Jefferson. Then she put Bobby into the other horse's stable for the night.

"Thank goodness you're doing the show ring," Reese whispered. She quickly washed and groomed Jefferson. "It keeps Mom off my back for a change."

Reese hadn't bothered to braid Jefferson's mane or tail for her events, even though her mom tried to talk her into it. "It's not worth it," Reese said. "No one in games is going to care what Jefferson's tail looks like."

"Must be nice," I muttered. Then I turned my attention back to Bobby. I had a show horse to finish getting ready.

* * *

On Saturday, I woke up bright and early for the Interschool Equestrian Competition. I had to finish getting myself and Bobby ready for the event.

I was completely exhausted. I felt like I'd been up all night.

As we pulled out of the driveway, my father waved goodbye in the early morning darkness. He'd promised to drive over to Woodside later if he had time. I wasn't really expecting him to show up.

My mother sat in the front seat of the SUV next to Mrs. Moriarty, who was driving. Reese and I both slumped in the back seat under blankets, still half-asleep. The horse trailer, with

Bobby and Jefferson secured inside, pulled along behind the SUV.

We drove up to Woodside just as the sun was starting to come up. The sky looked gray and threatening.

"Let's hope it doesn't rain," Mrs. Moriarty said as we pulled up. She backed the horse trailer up next to the yards that had been assigned to Ridgeview High.

I tried to stifle a yawn as I hopped out of the SUV. At the back of the horse trailer, I waited to help unload the horses. Reese already had the ramp down. She was inside the trailer, untying the two horses. Mrs. Moriarty carried a box full of grooming equipment from the car to Bobby's paddock.

My show class was the first event scheduled. Matt and Laura hadn't arrived yet. Reese still had plenty of time before she had to ride her dressage test.

Distracted, I glanced quickly at my watch. I had told Erica I would meet her at 7 a.m., and it was already 7:10.

"I'm going to run to the bathroom," I lied. "Be back in a minute." I hurried away before anyone from my team could object.

Mrs. Moriarty doesn't need my help anyway, I told myself. So far, Reese's mother had seemed happy for me to just stand there holding Bobby's lead while she did all the work.

My mother called out after me, but I pretended not to hear. It was easy to disappear in the rows of cars and trailers. We hadn't been the only ones to arrive early. The parking lot was filling up fast.

Erica was waiting for me on the other side of the grounds. Her dressage competition was being held in one of Woodside's huge indoor arenas. Lucky for me, the arena was far away and separate from the Interschool Equestrian Event.

Cadence was already saddled and waiting for me at Erica's trailer. Erica was busy studying her dressage test from a book with gold lettering on the cover. She looked up as I walked over.

"You're late," said Erica.

I mumbled something about traffic, but Erica was busy with the test. She hardly noticed my answer.

"I just need you to make sure Cadence has hay and water," Erica said, still looking at the book. "My first test is at 8:15. I'll see you here right away afterward."

I quickly filled a water bucket and a hay bag for Cadence. As I finished, Erica tossed the book into the front of the horse trailer. Then she untied Cadence.

I didn't hang around to watch Erica mount and ride off to warm up. Instead, I rushed back to my team's yards.

Mrs. Moriarty had transformed Bobby. While I was gone, he'd been brushed and polished so much that I hardly recognized him. His coat was gleaming. His hooves had been painted a glossy black. The neat braids in his mane and tail made him look elegant.

The Snyders had arrived while I was gone. My mother, holding a clipboard in her hand, was deep in conversation with Mr. Snyder. She was taking her role as team manager very seriously.

Matt and Laura were grooming their horses. Reese sat in her mother's car, learning her dressage test.

Mrs. Moriarty removed a saddle from the back of her car. I noticed that it was Reese's new dressage saddle.

"That's the wrong one," I said. "Mine is farther back." My own saddle was older and much more worn.

But Mrs. Moriarty ignored me. "This one will look better in the show ring," she said. "The judges will be looking for the most put-together horse in the ring. That includes the overall look of the horse and its rider. Now hurry up and get changed. Your class starts in five minutes."

I hurried over to one of the changing tents to put on my show outfit. I quickly changed out of the old jeans and T-shirt I had put on that morning. I'd needed to wear clothes that could get messy while I was taking care of the horses.

I put on a clean pair of khaki-colored jodhpurs with a white show shirt and matching stock tie. Mrs. Moriarty had pinned a silver stock pin engraved with an image of a horse head to my tie. I was also wearing a black show coat and black leather riding gloves. On my feet were a dressy pair of tall black riding boots.

Mrs. Moriarty had transformed Bobby and me. Almost everything we wore was borrowed.

Jefferson's high-quality tack added to Bobby's makeover, and I wore an expensive velvet riding helmet of Reese's.

Mrs. Moriarty had even managed to find ribbons in Ridgeview's school colors for Bobby's tail. I had ribbons in my hair too, which Mrs. Moriarty had pulled into a neat French braid.

When I finished changing, I hurried back over to where Mrs. Moriarty stood waiting with Bobby. She gave me a leg up. I settled into Reese's dressage saddle. I rode Bobby into the roped-off area that was the show ring. I was following the lead of the other riders. They were all walking and trotting around in a circle. Jessica trotted past on Ripple, but she didn't look at me.

Bobby and I both looked great. But I felt like an imposter. Reese's saddle felt weird. It wasn't as comfortable as my old, broken-in saddle.

I was too tired and worried about Erica to be excited about the makeover. And I certainly didn't feel like I could keep up with all the other girls in the ring. All of them, including Jessica, seemed so confident. On the other hand, I had no idea what I was supposed to be doing.

I sat up straight in the saddle. I tried to look like the others, but I was having a hard time concentrating.

By now, Erica's probably finished her dressage test, I thought as I rode in a circle. *She's probably wondering where I am.*

Nothing was working out like I'd planned. All I wanted now was for this day to be over.

There were dozens of riders in the show ring. All of them looked just as good as Bobby and I did. The judge, a young woman, was dressed in an elegant floral dress and a straw hat. I caught a glimpse of red hair, mostly hidden under the hat.

The judge stood in the middle of the show ring. She was directing the competitors to ride in a circle around her. She kept her eyes on one part of the circle, eyeing each horse and rider carefully as they rode past.

The judge called out instructions in a quiet, calm voice. "Trot, please," she called. Then she said, "Canter on."

Across the circle, I caught a glimpse of Jessica and Ripple. I noticed the judge giving them a second look. After only a few minutes, all of us were ordered to line up.

The judge raised her arm and pointed to several of the riders. Every time she pointed to someone, the pair would leave the circle and line up against the rope fence. I had no idea what was happening, but I didn't have to worry. The pointing finger never came my way.

"Everyone else, please line up on the end," the judge said as she began to walk back to the rope fence. Confused, I turned Bobby to follow the others.

The judge walked up and down the line. She stopped to inspect each horse. The other riders sat still on their horses. All eyes were on the judge, except for mine. My gaze kept wandering over to where I knew Erica would be. I was sure she was wondering where on earth I was.

After what seemed like forever, the judge stepped back away from the line. She looked at her notes for a moment. Then she pointed to a girl on a bay horse, who rode forward. Jessica was motioned forward next. She was followed by two girls from schools I had never heard of before.

I was desperate to leave the ring and find Erica. Instead, I had to wait politely with the rest of the riders while the judge presented ribbons to the four winning riders.

The girl on the bay was given the winning blue ribbon. Jessica placed second. Even though I was distracted, I noticed that Jessica didn't look too happy as the judge placed the red ribbon around Ripple's neck.

Jessica probably thought she was going to win, I thought.

Finally, the four ribbon winners rode a victory lap. Then the rest of us were allowed to leave.

I quickly dismounted and unsaddled. I put Bobby in his paddock. Then I made a swift exit before Mrs. Moriarty or my mother could stop me. Thankfully, I didn't see either of them standing near the yards.

They probably went to watch one of the other Ridgeview students ride, I thought. *I wish I had time to cheer my teammates on.*

When I arrived at the dressage arena, Erica was halfway through her test. I stood with some other spectators and watched. My boss and Cadence performed an impressive series of movements at walk, trot, and canter.

At the final halt, Erica reached down and gave Cadence a pat on the neck. She was smiling. I could tell she was happy with the young mare's performance.

Erica rode out of the dressage ring. She spotted me. Then she rode in my direction.

"That was great," I said. Erica dismounted and handed Cadence's reins to me. "You guys looked perfect out there."

But Erica didn't comment on her dressage test. Instead, she frowned. "You disappeared," she said, shaking her head. "I can't go looking for you every time I need your help, Annie. If you didn't want to come today, you should have just said so. I thought you'd be more reliable."

I felt my face get hot. I knew I was letting Erica down. But there was nothing I could do about it. Unable to meet Erica's steady gaze, I stared at a swirl in the hair on Cadence's neck.

"Um . . . I'm sorry, Erica," I said quietly. "I really am. There was something I had to do." I lifted my head and attempted a smile. "I'm here now, though. What do you need me to do?"

Erica checked her watch. "I have just enough time to get cleaned up before I start judging," she replied. "Can you walk Cadence for ten or fifteen minutes? Then put her away. Make sure she has enough hay to keep her busy, and refill her water bucket. My next test isn't until this afternoon. I'll see you back at Cadence's yard after lunch. Just make sure you check on her every now and then. Got it?"

I nodded. Erica walked away. She was heading toward the restrooms. I tugged lightly on Cadence's reins. The mare followed me.

"Come on, girl," I said. "Let's go get you some water."

I had until after lunch. That would give me enough time to get through the show-jumping round, at least.

I still needed to check to see what time my obstacle course was scheduled for. Maybe I could get the rest of my riding events over with.

Then Erica would never have to know about the mistake I had made.

I steered Cadence in the direction of the Ridgeview High yards. If I was careful, no one from my school would see me with Erica's horse. I could stay hidden among the horse trailers in the parking lot. I just wanted a quick peek.

"Annie!" someone yelled.

My heart sank at the sound of my father's voice. He had shown up after all, but at the worst possible time.

Of course he picks today of all days to show up, I thought miserably. *What else could go wrong?*

I turned to see my father. He was wearing a puzzled expression.

"This place is huge," my father said. "I've been wandering around looking for you and your mother. Who does that horse belong to? And where's your horse?"

I hesitated. What could I possibly say that wouldn't give everything away?

I looked across the parking lot. Through a gap in the horse trailers, I could see the Ridgeview High yards. My mother was holding Bobby. Someone had already tacked him up. This time, he was wearing my own saddle.

Mrs. Moriarty was there, too. I could see both of them looking around anxiously. I suddenly realized they were looking for me.

Oh, no, I thought. *Show jumping must be starting.*

Without another moment's hesitation, I shoved Cadence's reins into my father's hands. He looked startled.

"I'll explain later," I said. Then I took off, ducking and weaving between the cars and horse trailers. I had to get back to the Ridgeview High yards.

"What are you doing?" my father yelled after me. "What am I supposed to do with this horse? Come back here now!"

His voice held a hint of panic, but I didn't stop. I didn't have time to explain.

Breathless, I arrived at the paddock. I grabbed Bobby's reins from my mother.

"Annie, where on earth have you been?" my mother snapped. "We've been looking for you everywhere. You barely have enough time to warm up before your show-jumping round starts."

I ignored her. I just leaped onto Bobby's back. I kicked him into a trot. Then I rode off, leaving my mother and Mrs. Moriarty glaring after me.

"For goodness sake!" I heard Mrs. Moriarty say angrily.

The show-jumping round passed in a complete blur. Before I knew it, Bobby and I were finished. I rode out of the ring. I had no idea how we'd done.

I vaguely remembered hearing a sharp knock as Bobby's hooves hit one of the rails. I didn't think it fell, though. At that point, I was so stressed out that I really didn't care.

How did I get myself into this mess? I wondered.

I didn't dismount at the Ridgeview yards. Instead, I decided to ride Bobby straight back to find my father and Cadence. I figured we could swap horses while I took care of Cadence.

At this point, I seriously doubt things can get any worse, I thought.

But I was wrong.

Bobby and I arrived back at the horse trailers. My father was standing right where I had left him.

Cadence was nowhere to be seen.

I reined Bobby to a halt. All I could do was stare in horror at the empty space next to my father where Cadence should have been standing.

My father must have noticed my horrified expression. He quickly reassured me.

"You don't have to look so worried," he said cheerfully. "I didn't lose the horse. Erica came by and took her from me. Good thing she did, too. You know I don't know anything about horses. What were you thinking, leaving that horse here with me?"

As I stared at my father's puzzled face, I realized just how stupid I'd been.

How could I have thought I could help Erica and ride in a big competition on the same day? I thought. *This whole day has been a disaster.*

"I'm sorry, Dad," I said. My eyes filled with tears. I wiped them away with the back of my hand. "I did something really dumb," I said as I dismounted.

My fingers fiddled with the braids along Bobby's neck. I nervously poured the whole story out to my father.

He was more understanding than I'd expected. "Annie," he said with a sigh. "If the worst thing you ever do is try not to let people down, then you don't have a lot to worry about."

My father laid a comforting hand on my shoulder. He leaned down to look me in the eye. "I know I don't need to tell you that you should have been honest with everyone from the beginning," he said. "The only thing you can do now is damage control. You have to tell Erica and your team members what you did. I'm sure they'll understand when you explain."

"But I lied to everyone," I said quietly. The thought of telling to my friends, my mother, Mrs. Moriarty — and worst of all, Erica — what I'd done almost made me start crying again.

I winced a little as my father's usual sternness returned. "Yes, you did," he agreed. "And now all you can do is try to make things right. Come on, there's no time like the present. We'll start with your mother."

Pulling Bobby along behind me, I slowly followed my father toward the Ridgeview High yards to find my mother. I was not looking forward to this.

Mom and Mrs. Moriarty were standing beside an arena. They were watching Reese and Jefferson compete. They were in the middle of their dressage test. I put a finger to my lips, warning my father to be quiet and wait.

Reese's test was clean and accurate. I could tell by the look on Mrs. Moriarty's face that she was happy with her daughter's performance.

I was happy for my friend too. Even though I'd taken on too much work to actually enjoy the day, it was great to see Reese having a good time.

Reese came to her final halt and saluted the judge. The judge turned to speak to the man next to her, who was taking notes. She told him what comments he should write on the test score sheet.

Then the judge looked up. Her eyes met mine. I almost cried out in shock. It was Erica!

* * *

I put Bobby back in his paddock and promised my father that I would come straight back. Then I rushed off to check on Cadence.

Erica had returned the mare to her yard, where she stood quietly dozing. Her hay bag and water buckets were full. I used one of Erica's manure forks to scrape out a pile of manure. Then I left the mare in peace.

By the time I returned to my team's paddocks, Erica was there talking to the adults. My stomach clenched. Everyone was there. Mr. Snyder, Mrs. Moriarty, my parents, and my teammates.

Everyone was standing around relaxing. Both the dressage and show-jumping events were complete. That left games for my three teammates and the obstacle course for both Matt and me to do later in the afternoon.

"Ah, here she is," my father announced. Everyone turned to look at to me.

Erica was watching me expectantly. Unable to meet my boss's eye, I looked around the group.

I'd been hoping that my father had already spilled the beans about what I'd done. That would have saved me the embarrassment of having to tell everyone. It was obvious from their curious expressions, though, that my dad hadn't told them anything.

"I didn't know you were judging the show-jumping event, Erica," I began nervously.

"Neither did I, until last night," Erica replied. "One of the other judges had to cancel at the last minute. The organizers called me. They asked me to fill in."

My cheeks grew hot as I realized what that meant. "So you knew all along?" I asked quietly.

Erica nodded.

"Why didn't you say something?" I asked, looking up at her.

Erica shook her head. "It wasn't up to me," she told me. "You should have been honest with me from the beginning. It was a simple case of double-booking. It happens. All you had to do was tell me the truth."

"I'm really sorry, Erica," I said quietly. "Do you hate me?"

Erica laughed at that. "Of course I don't hate you," she said, putting her arm around me. "And I'll see you back at work next week, the same as usual. Just don't expect me to pay you for today. You've haven't exactly earned it."

I grinned in relief. Getting paid was the last thing I was worried about. The fact that Erica didn't hate me was enough. Keeping my job was a bonus.

Then my mother said, "Would someone please let the rest of us know what is going on?"

Erica smiled. "I think I'd better go check on Cadence," she said. "Annie, you're off the hook for the rest of the day. I'll see you at work on Monday afternoon."

"Okay, see you then. I really am sorry," I added.

Erica waved away the apology and walked off. I turned to face my mother and the others. I felt grateful when my father took a step forward to stand beside me.

"I owe you all an apology," I began. Then I explained what had happened.

When I finished my story, Mr. Snyder checked his watch. "Matt, Reese, and Laura," he said, "it's time for your games events. You'd better go saddle up." He looked at me for a second before turning to help the games riders.

"I'll talk to you at home," my mother said. I knew what that meant. I had a lecture and possible grounding coming up for sure.

Everyone is angry with me, I thought miserably. *Even Mr. Snyder.*

"Don't worry about Ray," a voice said from behind me. "He'll forget all about it by tomorrow. Your parents, too."

I turned around to find Mrs. Moriarty watching me.

"I think I owe you the biggest apology of all," I told Reese's mom. "You worked really hard to get Bobby ready. He looked amazing. And then I was too distracted to ride well. I'm so sorry I didn't win the show class."

Mrs. Moriarty smiled. "Oh, that's all right, Annie," she said. "I guess I had another reason for helping you. That Coulson woman always rubs me the wrong way. I should never have tried to use you to get back at her."

"Well, thanks for your help anyway," I said. "I appreciated it."

Mrs. Moriarty sighed. "You know, I've always wanted Reese to do well with her riding. I thought that meant winning lots of ribbons," she admitted. "But I've realized Reese couldn't care less whether she wins or not. She had a great

time today. We all did. Well, most of us, at least."
She smiled at me. "I guess it's just important to
just get in there and have fun. And don't bite off
more than you can chew!"

In the games area, Matt, Laura, and Reese were ready to ride in their next event. I looked over the equipment jealously. This was way more fun than riding in the show class.

Each rider had to take their horse through a sequence of games that had been set up by the event organizers. Just like in a team event, if a rider made a mistake in any game, he or she would have to turn back and correct it before going on. The rider with the fastest time would win.

There were three types of games. Each course was set up for the rider to go straight from one game to the next without stopping.

I watched a few riders from other schools run through the course. Then Matt and Bullet lined up for their turn. As the pair reached the starting line, I could tell Bullet knew this was the real thing. He started to fidget and then bounce up and down. Through it all, Matt sat calmly, holding Bullet in check.

Matt made it look so easy to ride a horse like Bullet. I knew it was very difficult to stay in the saddle while your horse was bouncing around like that.

The starter yelled, "Go!" They were off. Matt steered his horse through a set of bending poles at a fast gallop. Then he turned Bullet sharply on his haunches. They raced to pick a flag from the first barrel.

"Steady," Mr. Snyder muttered quietly.

My mom gripped my hand tightly. I gently pried her fingers away. She turned to smile at me apologetically. Then we both turned our attention back to Matt's ride.

By now, everybody's eyes were on Matt. He leaned over Bullet's neck, holding a flag in his left hand. Matt kept his eyes firmly on the second barrel as he approached. He neatly dropped the flag in the barrel. Then he galloped on without a backward glance.

The final game was stepping-stones. Matt dismounted and tiptoed across the stepping stones in one smooth motion. Before I could blink, he was vaulting back onto Bullet's back. Then they were flying across the finish line.

I knew his time would be hard to beat. Matt obviously thought so too. He was grinning widely as he rode up beside Mrs. Moriarty and me.

"It's Reese's turn," said Mrs. Moriarty. We saw Reese riding toward the starting line.

Matt suddenly let out a loud yell. Dozens of spectators looked over at us as he cheered for Reese. "Gooooo Reeeeese!" he hollered.

Reese looked up and grinned at us. She quickly flashed us a thumbs-up before turning her attention back to the course.

At the starter's signal, Reese and Jefferson flew through the course. Like Matt and Bullet, they made no errors, but I doubted they were as fast.

After they finished their runs, Matt and Reese rode straight to the obstacle course. We were scheduled to compete there in the last event of the day. I would have liked to watch Laura ride in the games, but I was competing in agility too. I had to hurry back and saddle Bobby for the event.

Matt, Reese, and I all had quiet horses with steady, easy-going personalities. Our horses made the obstacle course look easy. The horses stood quietly while we opened and closed gates. They walked over a bridge and negotiated trotting poles. They even let us carry a billowing coat from one point to another. And they did it all calmly and quickly.

When we were done, we all felt good about our performances during the day's events. We'd done our best.

Now, everybody was gathered around the scoreboards, waiting to see how we'd done in our events.

The Ridgeview High School uniforms mixed with uniforms from dozens of other schools. Parents and teachers were wandering around too.

I decided to get out of there. There were so many competitors in each event. It was crowded. Plus, my day had been distracted and hectic. I wasn't expecting a ribbon. And there was something else I needed to do. I headed toward the indoor arena for the second time that day.

I felt totally conspicuous in my school sweater and jodhpurs. The riders gathered there were all older. Many of them wore stylish black jackets, complete with tails that trailed down to the backs of their knees, and tall black leather boots.

I scanned the crowd, but I didn't see Erica. The screech of a microphone brought my attention to a small stage that had been set up in the middle of the dressage arena.

A low table was set up in front of the stage. Most of the table space was taken up with several enormous, glittering trophies — golden horses, looking elegant and regal with heads bowed and one foreleg raised in mid-air.

A man with white hair held the microphone. Beside him stood a woman wearing a large hat. She had a selection of different-colored sashes draped across her arm.

"Welcome all to this year's National Dressage Championships," the man began. "I'd like to thank everyone who came out to compete today. You all did an excellent job. Everyone should be very proud of themselves and their horses."

Just then, I spotted Erica on the other side or the ring. She was standing with a group of people I didn't know. They were all watching the man with the microphone.

"The winner of the Novice section this year goes to a pair with a big future," he continued. "Erica White and her stunning young mare, Cadence."

I clapped wildly while Erica accepted her sash and trophy. I knew how hard she and Cadence had trained. I was so proud of my boss.

I pushed my way past a line of people to reach Erica. "Congratulations!" I said breathlessly. "How cool is that?"

Erica transferred the big trophy into one hand and gave me a big hug. When she pulled back to look at me, she said, "I won't say thanks for your help."

For a second Erica's words stung. Then I noticed the spark of amusement in my boss's eye.

"I guess I deserved that," I said, still feeling embarrassed. "I promise I won't let you down like that next time."

"Next time!" Erica said, now laughing openly. "Next time I'll need a reliable groom. Someone who's actually around when I need help."

"You're right," I said, joining in on the teasing. "The one you had today wasn't much help at all, was she?"

Then Erica turned serious. "So, do you think my unreliable groom deserves a second chance?" she asked.

My eyes met Erica's. "I think everyone deserves a second chance," I said. "Don't you?"

Erica hugged me again. "I do," she agreed. "I definitely do."

I left Erica to finish celebrating with her friends. I headed back to the Ridgeview yards to find my team. Reese, Matt, and Laura spotted me as I walked up.

"Fourth place!" Matt yelled. He and the two girls gathered around me. I looked to Reese for confirmation.

"Can you believe it?" Reese said, grinning. "Our first time as a team, too. Swindley came in second. Crayton High got first place."

"Wow," I said. I was stunned. Winning a team ribbon was something I had secretly hoped for, but I'd never dreamed it would actually happen. "How did we manage that?" I asked.

"Matt won his games division and got a third in the show jumping," said Reese. "And Laura came second in her dressage class. Plus she got second in games."

"What about you?" I asked Reese.

"She did great," Laura cut in. "Third in the obstacle course and fourth in dressage."

I wanted to be happy for my friends, but it wasn't easy knowing I'd let the team down.

Who knows how much better we might have done if I'd been giving my full attention to my riding today? I thought.

"So where did I end up?" I asked quietly. I was almost afraid to hear the answer.

"Well you already know you didn't place in the show ring," Reese told me. "And you just missed getting a ribbon on the obstacle course. You were only a few seconds behind."

"Oh," I said, trying to smile. Inside though, I was disappointed. When nobody said anything about show jumping, I didn't see any point in asking about it. Obviously, I hadn't placed.

"Come on," said Matt. "The award presentations are about to start. I don't want to miss anything!"

At the awards ceremony, the parents of the Ridgeview team members gathered around to congratulate us. Nearby, I saw Mrs. Coulson and the rest of the Swindley team standing in a group. Jessica glanced my way with a smug expression. Mrs. Coulson was holding her daughter's second-place ribbon for the show event.

Seeing that, I felt guilty. Mrs. Moriarty had gone to so much trouble to make Bobby and me look good for the show. I wished I could have at least placed to help make up for all the work she'd done.

Austin left the Swindley group and walked over to us to shake hands with everyone. After a second or two, Jessica joined us.

"Look out next year," said Laura. "The Ridgeview team is going to be a force to be reckoned with."

"Hmm . . . I don't know about that," said Austin jokingly. "I can't really see it."

Everyone laughed at that, even Jessica.

The crowd grew quiet as an older woman, looking a little out of place in a blue floral dress, stepped up to the microphone. She introduced herself as the event coordinator and thanked everyone for coming. Then she began to announce the team results and the individual winners.

I watched my mother, as team manager, proudly accept the small fourth-place trophy Ridgeview had won. One by one, my team members and the winners from other schools walked to the front of the crowd to receive their individual ribbons.

The announcer called Matt's name. He walked up to collect his third-place ribbon for show jumping.

I stopped paying close attention to the announcements for second place since I already knew how everyone else had done. Then Reese nudged me.

"And finally, in first place for show jumping, Annie Boyd from Ridgeview High," the event coordinator announced.

Somebody patted me on the back and pushed me forward. I walked forward in a daze and accepted my ribbon while Reese, Matt and Laura cheered and whistled.

I couldn't believe I'd won first place in show jumping. But the surprises weren't over yet.

Mrs. Davies suddenly appeared beside the event coordinator. I stared, open-mouthed. I hadn't expected the school principal to show up.

Mrs. Davies spoke briefly to the event coordinator. Then she turned to face the crowd.

"Before everyone leaves for the day I have a quick announcement," she began. "I'd like everyone to know about a very special initiative started by one of our Ridgeview High team members. At the suggestion of Annie Boyd, our team recruited other students to sponsor them for this event. They're planning to donate the money they raised from those sponsorships to charity."

Mrs. Davies paused while the crowd turned to the Ridgeview team and clapped. I blushed with embarrassment. I wasn't used to being the center of attention.

"I'm very proud of our team for their hard work," Mrs. Davies said. "I think it's a wonderful idea, and I'd like to ask all of the other schools to consider doing something similar next year."

Matt poked me in the ribs. "See what you did?" he teased. "Now we'll have to raise money every year, whether we want to or not."

But I wasn't paying attention to Matt. I was focused on the sight of my father, who had just walked up beside Mrs. Davies.

"I have two checks here," my father began. He looked down at the two slips of paper he was holding. "One of them is for the sponsorship money raised by my daughter, Annie, and her friends."

Everyone in the crowd turned to look at me.

"The other check, I am proud to say, is being donated by Ridgeview Real Estate," my father continued. "Annie, would you please come up and name the charity that will be receiving the fundraising money?"

I met my father's eyes, and he gave me a wink. He was full of surprises. I walked forward to join my father onstage and accepted the check he held out to me.

I didn't really think this through, I realized. *What's the best charity to donate the money to? I have to say something.*

"Ummm," I mumbled.

"Speak up," my father said in a loud whisper that made the crowd laugh.

A name suddenly popped into my head. I'd had a charity in mind all along, I remembered.

"I'd like the money to go to Hopedale Horse Rescue," I said clearly.

Everyone in the crowd clapped. Teachers and parents nodded in approval. A few boys whistled.

I looked up at my father and smiled. It looked like everything had turned out all right after all.

* * *

That evening, I turned Bobby out in his paddock at home. It had been a long day. We were both exhausted. All I wanted now was to go up to my room and crawl into bed.

I turned to close the gate. My father was standing there.

"How are the sheep?" he asked.

I really hadn't noticed. "They're fine," I replied. I hesitated for a moment. Then I added, "Thanks for the sponsorship, Dad. I really appreciate it. But I thought you weren't going to ask Mr. Snyder this year."

"Oh, well, I changed my mind. Besides, community involvement is always good for business," he said gruffly.

"Right," I said. I tried to hide how disappointed his answer made me feel.

Why can't he ever do something just for me? I thought angrily. With a loud sigh, I turned and went inside the house. I left my father standing at the gate.

"What's the matter?" my mother asked as I came in.

I threw her an angry look. "It's Dad," I said. "Everything's always about work. He never cares about me."

"That's not true," my mother said. She carefully stirred her tea. "Your father is very proud of you. He told me so."

"He is?" I asked, surprised.

"Of course he is, Annie," my mother said. "You have good grades, a job, and new friends. And he thinks you show a lot of responsibility by taking such good care of Bobby."

"So why doesn't he ever tell me those things himself?" I asked.

"Don't be too hard on him, Annie," my mother replied. "He does his best."

I made my way back outside, still thinking about what my mother had said.

Maybe Mom is right, I thought. *After all, Dad did show up today. That's something. And he came through for me with the donation. Maybe he just has a hard time telling me he's proud of me.*

I walked back up to the paddock. My father was still leaning on the gate and watching Bobby and the sheep as they grazed.

"You know, Annie," my father said as I walked over to stand next to him, "you're going to need a bigger horse someday. Especially if you plan to keep competing in these different events."

I leaned against the fence and gazed out at Bobby in his paddock.

"Not for a long time, Dad," I said. "Besides, I'm happy with Bobby."

I paused and thought for a minute. "But if you wanted to get yourself a horse, I'd be more than happy to teach you how to ride," I said innocently, trying not to laugh.

My father looked down at me in surprise. He must have noticed my face. "Brat," he growled affectionately.

Then he reached out to my shoulders and hugged me close to him.

About the Author

When she was growing up, Bernadette Kelly desperately wanted her own horse. Although she rode other people's horses, she didn't get one of her own until she was an adult. Many years later, she is still obsessed with horses. Luckily, she lives in the country, where there is plenty of room for her four-legged friends. When she's not writing or working with her horses, Bernadette and her daughter compete at riding club competitions.

Horse Tips from Bernadette

⊙ Horses need regular health care. Every six to eight weeks, your horse's hooves should be trimmed and its shoes checked.

⊙ As a rider, you're the one teaching your horse. Horses can pick up bad habits just as quickly as good ones, so make sure you're teaching him correctly.

⊙ Be gentle and try not to cause your horse pain while riding.

⊙ Horses are much stronger than you, so always be careful.

For more, visit Bernadette's website at
www.bernadettekelly.com.au/horses

Glossary

- **conspicuous** (kuhn-SPIK-yoo-uhss)—stands out and can be seen easily

- **dressage** (dress-AHJ)—the art of riding and training a horse

- **embarrassment** (em-BA-ruhss-mint)—the feeling of being awkward and uncomfortable

- **girth** (GURTH)—a band that buckles to the saddle and passes underneath the horse's stomach to hold the saddle in place

- **groom** (GROOM)—someone who takes care of horses

- **grudge** (GRUHJ)—a feeling of resentment toward someone who has hurt or insulted you in the past

- **jodhpurs** (JOD-purz)—pants worn for horseback riding

- **paddock** (PAD-uck)—an enclosed area where horses can graze or exercise

- **sponsor** (SPON-sur)—to give money and support to people who are doing something worthwhile, often for charity

- **Thoroughbred** (THUR-oh-bred)—a breed of English horses developed especially for racing

Dear Annie,

I agreed to babysit for a neighbor this weekend, but I also made plans to help my friend with a project for school. I totally forgot they were on the same day! Now I'm supposed to be in two places at once. What do I do? Help!

Sincerely,

Double-Booked in Dallas

Dear Double-Booked in Dallas,

Don't panic! Everyone makes mistakes sometimes. Even the most organized people can double-book themselves. Start by being honest about your mistake.

Here are some double-booking tips:

1. **Recognize the problem.** To start, realize that you can't be in two places at once. You'll have to make a decision.

2. **Be honest.** Hiding the problem won't help. Tell your friend and neighbor what happened. Explain the mix-up. Chances are, they'll be understanding.

3. **Apologize.** Tell both parties involved you're sorry about your mistake. Ask what you can do to make it up to them.

4. **Find a solution.** Maybe your friend can help you babysit, or you can work on her project when you're done. Be creative with your problem-solving.

Think about getting a planner or calendar to schedule your commitments. That'll prevent you from double-booking again! Love,

Annie

Use these reading group questions when you and your friends discuss this book.

1. Talk about Annie's decision to try to attend both her own competition and Erica's dressage event. Do you think she made the right choice? What else could she have done?

2. Annie and her friends are determined to organize a team for the Interschool Equestrian Competition. Talk about a time you helped organize a team or group of some kind. What was it for? How did you go about starting it? What difficulties did you experience in doing so?

3. Annie has to compete against some of her friends from the riding club at the Interschool event. Have you ever had to compete against a friend? How did you handle it?

The Ridgeview Book Club Journal Prompts

A journal is a private place to record your thoughts and ideas. Use these prompts to get started. If you like, share your writing with your friends.

1. Have you ever had a conflict between two commitments and had to choose just one? Write about a time when you had to make a choice and felt like you were letting someone else down. How did you deal with your decision?

2. Relationships with parents can be difficult sometimes. Write about your relationship with one or both of your parents. What makes it special? What makes it hard?

3. Write about a cause you're dedicated to. Is It a charity or a different type of organization? What is the mission or purpose and why is it important to you? What inspired you to get involved?

Join the Ridgeview
Riding Club!

Read all of Annie's
adventures.

RIDGEVIEW RIDING CLUB

Heads
or
Tails?
by Bernadette Kelly

SPORTS FICTION

RIDGEVIEW RIDING CLUB

Making
Waves
by Bernadette Kelly

SPORTS FICTION

RIDGEVIEW RIDING CLUB

Taking a
Break
by Bernadette Kelly

SPORTS FICTION